The Feelings Book

Todd PARR

Megan Tingley Books
LITTLE, BROWN AND COMPANY
New York   Boston

Little, Brown and Company

Hachette Book Group
1290 Avenue of the Americas, New York, NY 10104
Visit our website at www.lb-kids.com

Little, Brown and Company is a division of Hachette Book Group, Inc.
The Little, Brown name and logo are trademarks of Hachette Book Group, Inc.

The publisher is not responsible for websites (or their content) that are not owned by the publisher.

First Paperback Edition: April 2009
Originally published in hardcover in September 2000 by Little, Brown and Company.

Library of Congress Cataloging-in-Publication Data

Parr, Todd.
  The feelings book / Todd Parr. — 1st ed.
     p. cm.
Summary: Children express different moods, including "I feel very mad,"
"I feel like reading books all day," and "I feel like wearing funny underwear."
[1. Emotions—Fiction.]   I. Title
 PZ7. P2447Fe 2000
 [E]—dc21   99-42775
 ISBN 978-0-316-04346-5

20 19 18 17 16 15 14 13 12 11

IM

Printed in China

This book is dedicated to
Dad, Tammy, Sandy, Sara, Dawn, Bryan, Bill,
Candy, Jerry, Liz and Gerry, John and Linda
Alioto, Maggie W., Jeff and Steve, Jim and
Jean, Bully, Mow, Isabel and Benny, Michael,
Artt, Megan, Cindy Sue, Kerri, Stacey, Linda,
and everyone at Little, Brown.

Love,
Todd

Sometimes I feel silly

Sometimes I feel cranky

Sometimes I feel scared

EEK

Sometimes I feel like standing on my head

Sometimes I feel like reading
a book under the covers

Sometimes I feel like celebrating my birthday

even though
it's not today

Sometimes I feel brave

Sometimes I feel like looking out the window all day

Sometimes I feel

like dancing

Sometimes I feel
like making mudpies

Sometimes I feel like
I have a tummy ache

Sometimes I feel like holding hands with a friend

Sometimes I feel lonely

Sometimes I feel like yelling really loud

Sometimes I feel like staying in the bathtub all day

Sometimes I feel like trying something new

Sometimes I feel like dressing up

Sometimes I feel

like doing nothing

Sometimes I feel like camping with my dog

Sometimes I feel
like crying

Sometimes I feel like eating pizza for breakfast

Sometimes I feel
like a king

No matter how you feel, don't keep your feelings to yourself. Share them with someone you love.

Love,
Todd